Artlist Collection
THE DOG™

A Star Is Born

D0033716

By Howie Dewin

SCHOLASTIC INC.

New York   **Toronto**   **London**   **Auckland**
Sydney   **Mexico City**   **New Delhi**   **Hong Kong**

For
AD
BS
ME
&
MA

ISBN-13: 978-0-545-11541-4
ISBN-10: 0-545-11541-8

© 2009 artlist

12 11 10 9 8 7 6 5 4 3 2 1   9 10 11 12 13/0

Designed by Deena Fleming
Printed in the U.S.A.
First printing, September 2009

GO TO

Meet Curley

Curley the Poodle lives at the Fabulous Fur Beauty Salon. Every show dog in town comes to Fabulous Fur to prepare for the Best in Show competition. But it's not easy for Curley. Everyone says, "Curley is the nicest dog in the world!" But nobody ever says, "Curley is a *beauty*!" Could there be a show dog inside Curley waiting to come out?

Chapter 1

It was early Monday morning. A new week was beginning at the Fabulous Fur Beauty Salon. Felicia, the salon owner, was busy in the back room.

"Ready for another day, Miss Curley?" asked Felicia.

Curley the Poodle sat on the styling table. The table was where the beautiful show dogs sat when Felicia groomed them. Curley loved early morning. It was peaceful in the salon and she had Felicia all to herself. Once the front door opened, Felicia noticed only the show dogs.

"You're a good dog, aren't you, Curley?" Felicia said. Curley yipped. She wanted to be a good dog. But she wanted to be a beautiful dog, too. She dreamed of the day when Felicia would say, "You're a beautiful dog, aren't you, Curley?" But it didn't seem like that day would ever happen.

"Get down, Curley," Felicia said. "It's time to—"

BANG! BANG!

"What is that?" Felicia cried.

Curley ran to the front of the store. She knew people didn't think of Poodles as guard dogs, but Curley knew that they could be. She took her job seriously.

BANG! BANG!

"Just a minute!" called Felicia.

Felicia rushed to the front door. She pulled up the shade and turned the lock. The door flung open.

"Good morning!" cried a woman being led by a big white Standard Poodle. The dog was Pretty Patty and her look-alike owner was Elaine.

Of course it's Elaine! thought Curley. *Who else would be that impatient?*

"Here we are!" Elaine sang out. "Patty the

Pretty Poodle has arrived! And so has show week!"

"It certainly has!" Felicia said with a smile.

Curley admired how patient Felicia acted with her customers. Sometimes they seemed a bit silly to Curley. But Felicia always took them seriously. This week her customers would be extra silly. That's because this was the week of the dog show. It wasn't a big deal for anybody who didn't live in their county. But for the dog owners who *did* live here, it was a *very big* deal!

"It's a big week for us," Elaine said in a high-pitched voice. "This is Pretty Patty's year. I just know it is! If this dog isn't a Best in Show just waiting to happen, I don't know who is!"

Elaine stared at Patty. She adored her dog. Curley watched and tried not to feel jealous. That was how she wanted Felicia to look at her.

"We need to schedule everything! Don't we, my itty-bitty pretty Poodle?" Elaine kissed Patty's nose again and again.

Itty-bitty? Curley said to herself. *Patty is the biggest Poodle I've ever seen!*

Curley was not big. In fact, she was small for a Standard Poodle, but too big for a Miniature Poodle. She didn't fit anywhere.

"Shampoo. Brushing. Nails. Ears. Pom-poms. Crimping . . ." Elaine was listing all the things that had to be done.

I'm a bit small.

"Okay," said Felicia. "Let's make a plan."

This was Curley's cue. It was time for Curley to make Patty comfortable while the humans did their people things. Curley's job was to keep the beautiful dogs happy while they waited for their treatments.

What Makes a Good Show Dog?

In the world of dog shows, each breed has its own set of rules. Those rules say how big a dog must be and what fur colors are allowed in that breed. The rules even talk about how the head and body should be shaped. But a good show dog must also have the right attitude. Just like people, some dogs like to perform and some don't. A good show dog likes being in the spotlight!

"Would you like something to drink?" Curley asked Patty.

"Do you have anything distilled?" asked Patty. "I drink only special water."

"Of course," Curley said.

She led Patty to an empty bowl. She stepped on a pedal and fresh water filled the bowl.

"You're looking fit today, Patty," Curley said. "Are you excited about the show this week?"

"I'm a wreck, if you must know," Patty said. Patty was fragile. It was easy to upset her. So Curley changed the subject.

"Did you see that new cat who moved in next door?" Curley asked. "He sits in the window."

"I was looking at myself in the window," Patty said. She started to drink.

Curley stole a glance at Felicia. Felicia was staring at Patty. Curley knew that show dogs were Felicia's business. No matter what she did, Curley would never be a show dog. She just wasn't born with those kinds of looks.

It was three in the afternoon when Curley

heard the front door opening.

"*Lydia!*" Curley barked.

This was her second favorite time of day.

"Hey there, Curley!" called ten-year-old Lydia. "How has your day been?"

Lydia came to the salon every day after school. It was her job to sweep and do other chores. But she was also Curley's biggest fan.

"You look cuddly today!" Lydia said. She knelt down to give Curley a hug. Then she whispered in Curley's ear, "If I have time, I'll give you a little brush and make you extra fluffy, too! Okay?"

"Yes!" yipped Curley. She licked Lydia on the nose.

"Stop!" Lydia giggled. "Now let's get busy!"

Just then, a huge bang sounded behind them. Lydia and Curley spun around.

The front door had swung all the way open. A giant dog stood in the middle of the room.

He looks like one huge muscle! Curley thought.

"C-c-can I h-h-help you?" Curley whimpered.

The enormous dog didn't move. He just curled his lip.

There are three types of Poodle: toy, miniature, and standard. The types are distinguished by adult shoulder height.

Chapter 2

Curley held as still as she could. She could feel Lydia standing slowly. The huge dog remained frozen . . . until suddenly – he broke out in rhyme.

"You see me shine,

You see me strut,

You see me pass by all those mutts.

'Cause I'm Lionel,

The Rott-weil-er,

Best in Show, to be sure!"

Curley's mouth fell open. Patty turned her head away in disgust.

"Lionel!" a voice boomed at the front door. "Stand tall and don't talk to the little people." A man with as many muscles as Lionel stood in the doorway of the salon.

"We are here to schedule all necessary

Best in Show,
to be sure!

treatments for the Grand Champion. The show begins on Friday, and Lionel must be ready. He will be collecting his sixth Best in Show trophy.

"I am Dennis," the man said to Felicia. He strutted over to the front desk. Lionel followed Dennis's lead. He took another strut around the waiting room. He repeated his chant more quietly. His head was held high.

"'Cause I'm Lionel,
The Rott-weil-er,
Best in Show, to be sure!"

"Let's go," Dennis said. He stepped right in front of Elaine. Elaine gasped in surprise.

"Get a good look, Poodle Girl?" Lionel snarled at Patty. Patty gasped just like Elaine.

Lydia quietly stepped in front of Patty. She took Curley and Patty into a corner, but the Rottweiler continued to strut. He circled the room, waiting for someone to stare at him.

"He is a good-looking dog," Curley finally muttered.

"How dare you!" Patty snapped.

"Well, not like you, Patty," Curley stumbled. "No one is as beautiful as you!"

"Pardon me!" snapped Elaine at the front desk. "I was here first."

Dennis turned and looked at Elaine. It was like he'd never seen her before. He started to laugh.

"You have Poodle hair, lady!" He pointed to the pom-poms that sat on both sides of Elaine's head.

Lydia gasped and covered her mouth.

Elaine let out a low growl.

Do People Really Look Like Their Dogs?

Some people really do resemble their dogs. Sometimes they have the same hair color. Sometimes they have similar expressions. In fact, there are contests around the country with names such as "I Look Like My Dog!" It's fun to keep a lookout for people and dogs who might win that contest!

She really is like her dog, thought Curley.

Elaine snarled. It looked she was going to nip Dennis on the arm.

"Okay!" cried Felicia. "Everyone relax. We have plenty of time to get everybody ready!"

Lionel was still circling. He stopped in front of Patty and Curley.

"It's a good thing I'm smart, too," Lionel hissed. "Otherwise I couldn't count how many times I've been BEST IN SHOW. Luckily, I can count! Five! Oh, yeah! That's right. F-I-V-E. Five times."

"Well, you might not have to learn how to count to six," Patty finally snapped. She couldn't take it anymore.

Ready to win again!

"It's not worth it," Curley whispered to Patty. "Don't even talk to him."

But Patty couldn't stop herself. "This year, you'll have to beat me to get Best in Show!"

"Ha!" Lionel laughed. "And that's a problem for me—why?"

"I said, step back!" Elaine's voice was loud

and high-pitched, like a dog yipping. "You cannot take that appointment! I have that appointment!"

"Look, lady," Dennis said. "I have these." He pulled out a long chain. There were five shiny medals attached to it. "Mine is the only show dog in the room. We get what we want."

Felicia put her hands between the two. "I have scheduled you both. Look at the calendar and see when you're coming in. I've written all your appointments on this card. I don't want to hear another word!"

Curley looked at Felicia. She was so proud of her. She was good at her job. Curley felt lucky to have a human like Felicia.

"You don't have a hope of taking my trophy." Lionel was still snapping at Patty.

Curley felt like she had to do her job now. Felicia had done such a good job with the humans. Curley had to do the same with the dogs.

"Well, I think you're both going to make the competition exciting to watch!" Curley announced to both dogs.

They turned to look at Curley. For a minute they were quiet. Curley had done it!

Then Patty said to Lionel, "If you and your human don't cheat again this year, I have a good chance."

Suddenly, the two dogs were locked in a stare down. They both growled so low that only Curley could hear it.

"Take it back!" Lionel hissed. His jaws were an inch from Patty's neck.

Poodles are one of the oldest breeds, and have been popular throughout Europe for several hundred years.

Chapter 3

"Okay!" Curley exclaimed. She ran to the bucket by the front desk. "Rawhide chips all around!"

Curley bravely stepped between the two dogs. She dropped a rawhide chip for each of them.

"Good for the teeth!" Curley said cheerfully. "No champion is ready without rawhide!"

The two show dogs took a step back from each other. Their eyes darted toward the chips.

"Come on, folks," Curley said in a calm tone. "You are both beautiful and talented dogs. I feel lucky to know you."

Patty let out a silly giggle. Lionel looked at Curley.

"I can understand how you might feel that

way," Lionel said. "Thanks for the chip, kid."

The two beautiful dogs settled down to gnaw on their rawhide.

Which Breeds Get Along with Which Breeds?

The breed of a dog is not the most important thing when two dogs are being introduced to each other. It's more important that each dog is well trained. It's also important that they have been taught how to socialize (just like people). There is a better chance that two dogs will get along if they are introduced when they are young. Of course, it also depends on the individual dog. Some dogs are just plain friendlier than other dogs—no matter what kind of breed!

"These are the appointments I want!" Dennis placed a list in front of Felicia. "This is the order in which I want the treatments. And this is the exact schedule they must follow."

Dennis ignored Elaine's horrified expression.

"I'm sure you'd like to hang Lionel's picture in your window," Dennis said. He smiled at Felicia. "You could say you groomed the *six*-time Best in Show. Are you going to tell me that wouldn't be good for your business?"

Felicia could hear Elaine sputtering in disgust. But Felicia didn't look up from her date book. She compared Dennis's list to her date book.

"Well, it appears that I can schedule these dates," Felicia said.

Curley could tell that Felicia wasn't happy. She was putting on her "happy customer" face.

Felicia handed the list back to Dennis. "We will see you back here tomorrow," she said. But Curley knew it wasn't her friendly voice.

"Lionel! My champion! Let us depart!"

Dennis announced.

Lionel stood. He swaggered over to Dennis.

"I've had enough of those two," Lydia whispered into Curley's ear.

Just then, Patty stepped out from behind the desk.

Curley saw Dennis's expression change in an instant. It was like he'd never actually looked at Patty before.

"Who's that?" Dennis demanded. He seemed nervous.

"I beg your pardon," snipped Elaine. "Stay away from my dog. That is Pretty Patty. She doesn't need to know the likes of you!"

"Your dog? Since when? I've never seen that dog before."

"You most certainly have. She was a puppy last year. And you have seen her mother and her grandmother. Patty comes from a *lo-o-o-ng* line of champions!"

Dennis stared at the Poodle. Then he turned away. Curley could tell he was trying to act like he didn't care.

"Patty will be Best in Show by the end of this weekend. You mark my words!"

Dennis laughed, but it didn't sound real.

"Lionel!" he snapped. "Let's go!"

The two bullies left the shop without looking back.

Everyone let out a sigh of relief.

"Come on, Curley," Lydia said. "Let's get to our work."

Curley and Lydia headed into the back room. Felicia finished up with Elaine. At last the day seemed to be getting back to normal.

An hour later, Felicia was combing out a Collie named Shine. Lydia was sweeping up around the tables. Curley was dancing around and keeping Shine amused.

Ring! The bell that hung above the front door sounded.

"Now who could that be?" asked Felicia. "We don't have anyone else on the schedule."

She put down her combs and walked out front. Curley followed her just to make sure she was safe. But by the time they got to the front desk, the door had opened and closed again. Whoever had come in was gone.

"I didn't leave this open," Felicia said quietly. She was looking at her date book. Then she looked up and down the street.

Curley stretched up. She put her front paws on the desk. The appointment book was sitting open like someone had been studying all the appointments for this week.

Poodles are retrievers, or bird dogs, developed to assist hunters in finding and retrieving game.

Chapter 4

"It's going to be another crazy day, Curley!" Felicia said the next morning. "But I know you'll be right there to help me!" She gave Curley a quick pat on the head. Then she unlocked the door, and the day began.

All morning, beautiful dogs paraded in and out of the store. Felicia combed and trimmed them. She painted toenails. She made fluffy tails fluffier.

Curley kept the dogs company. She brought them treats. She made sure they had water.

At lunchtime, Felicia sat down hard on her chair. "Whew! I'm already tired, and the day is only half over!"

Curley ran to Felicia's side. Then she tugged on a stool nearby. She pulled hard until it was in front of Felicia's chair. Felicia smiled. She lifted her feet. Curley gave the stool one more push. Felicia lowered her feet and sighed.

"You're so good to me, Curley!" she said. "How did I ever get so lucky to have the perfect assistant? How will I ever repay you?"

Tell me I'm beautiful, Curley thought. Then the little dog felt a wave of sadness. But she didn't want Felicia to know how she felt. That might make Felicia feel sad. So she yipped happily and trotted out of the room.

Curley headed to her secret place. Whenever she needed some quiet or a place to feel sad,

she knew just where to go. Behind the store's back door was an alley. There were fire escapes and trash cans. There was a big metal box that made lots of noise when the air conditioner was on. There was the box that had all the switches that made the lights go on and off.

But what Curley liked were lots of little corners. They made perfect hiding places. Curley always went to the corner farthest from the salon's back door. Curley turned around three times and settled down for a little nap. She would sleep for only a few minutes. But then she would be ready for the afternoon.

BANG! BANG!

Curley had just closed her eyes when she heard loud noises coming from the shop. She jumped up and ran back inside.

"Let's go!" boomed a big voice.

Curley knew just who it was. Lionel and Dennis had arrived.

"The champion has arrived!" Dennis announced loudly. "Let's get busy!"

Lionel was strutting around the room. He

stopped every few steps to pose. Curley took a deep breath and went to work.

"It's nice to see you, Lionel," Curley said politely.

"Did someone say something?" Lionel said in a tired voice.

"Down here," Curley replied. She smiled nicely.

"Oh, right, the little servant dog," Lionel muttered. "How are you doing, kid?"

"Can I get you anything?" Curley asked.

"A trophy," Lionel sneered. "Oh, never mind. I'll have another one of those by the weekend."

Every time Lionel opened his mouth, Curley wanted Patty to win even more.

"All right, then," said Felicia.

Curley could hear the tension in her voice.

"Let's go to work. Come with me, Lionel."

Lionel and Felicia headed to the back room. Dennis followed so he could keep telling everyone what to do. Curley waited until they were all settled. Then she slipped back out to her hiding place. It was impossible to be nice to

Lionel for long.

One of the things Curley liked about her spot in the back alley was that she could still hear everything that happened in the shop.

"We'll start with a shampoo," Felicia said. "Then we'll go from there."

Best in Show

There are many different kinds of dog shows. Some are big national events with thousands of dogs competing. Some are small local shows where there might just be a certain breed competing. In big dog shows, Best in Show is an award given when lots of different breeds are competing. The winner of each breed then competes for Best in Show. But there are also lots of small-town shows with their own rules. The show in Curley's town is like that!

"I'm fine with that," Dennis said. "Just be sure you're using the shampoos I requested. I'm going to step out for a minute, but I'll be back."

"Take all the time you need!" Felicia said cheerfully. Curley could tell that she was happy that Dennis was leaving.

Curley heard the bell over the front door ring as Dennis left. Just knowing that Dennis was gone made Curley feel better. Lionel was a show-off, but Dennis was a bully. Curley didn't like it when the man was around.

Curley finally fell into a nice afternoon nap. She was dreaming of Felicia putting her on the grooming table. Felicia looked at her like she was the most beautiful dog she'd ever seen.

Then something jingled.

Suddenly, Curley was awake. A flash of something bright filled the alley. Then she heard another jingling sound. Curley didn't move a muscle.

Someone was moving in the alley. She saw another flash. It was like sunlight catching a piece of metal. Curley realized the metal thing was hanging from the back pocket of the person in the alley. Someone was standing right by the box with the switches that made the lights go on and off.

It was Dennis! Dennis had gone in the front door and snuck around to the back alley.

Why was he looking at the box with the switches?

Chapter 5

"Climb up," Lydia said.

Curley was hoping she would say that. It was the middle of the week. The salon was always quieter then. This was when Felicia caught up on paperwork.

Lydia and Curley had the back room to themselves. That meant one important thing to Curley. It meant Lydia might decide to play beauty salon on Curley.

"You know I think you're the most beautiful dog in the world, don't you, Curley?" Lydia said.

The little Poodle wagged her tail. She licked Lydia's hand. She did know. Lydia was always telling her she was a beautiful Poodle.

"You are a unique beauty, Curley," Lydia said. "Do you know what that means? It means nobody else is beautiful like you. It's the best way to be beautiful. It means that nobody else can compare to you!"

You are beautiful, too, Lydia, Curley barked softly.

Sometimes Curley thought Lydia needed someone to tell her she was beautiful, too. There were days when Lydia seemed really sad. Curley didn't know a lot about Lydia. She had been hanging around the salon for months and gradually started helping out. But Curley only knew the little things Lydia whispered to her.

Lydia first came into the salon with a stray dog. Curley remembered how surprised Felicia looked when Lydia came through the door. She had a scraggly dog with her. It wasn't the kind of dog that usually came for grooming.

"May I help you?" Felicia had asked Lydia.

"My name is Lydia," the girl said. She seemed nervous. "I live down the block. My mom and I have a small apartment, and she says I can't keep this dog."

Curley could still remember the tears in Lydia's eyes.

"He's been living in the park," Lydia said. Her voice wavered. "He really needs a home. I love him, but I'm not allowed . . . I was wondering . . ."

Felicia had been really nice to Lydia. It was one of the things Curley loved about Felicia. She always tried to help people. Felicia helped Lydia find a good shelter for the dog. She made sure Lydia knew when the dog got adopted. She also offered Lydia a job. Since then, Lydia came almost every day after school. She swept the floors and helped keep things neat.

"You can make friends with Curley," Felicia had suggested.

Curley would never forget the look Lydia had given her. The first time Lydia looked at Curley, they both knew they'd be good friends.

Lydia put her hand on Curley's head. It brought the Poodle back to the present.

"I think we should try some red bows today," Lydia said to Curley. "We've never tried red on you. It might just be your best color!"

My best color, thought Curley. *If only Felicia would walk in on us. If she could just see that I can be beautiful, too. I need just a little grooming like everyone else.*

Grooming a Show Dog

Preparing a dog to compete in a show takes lots of work. A professional groomer washes and dries the fur. They might use all kinds of gels and conditioners to make the fur extra shiny or fluffy. Sometimes they clip or shave the fur in a certain style depending on the breed. But it's not just the fur that counts. Groomers take care of nails, paws, eyes, ears, and just about anything else you can think of!

Just then the front door bell jingled.

"Uh-oh!" said Lydia. "Beauty time is over!"

Lydia quickly lowered Curley to the floor. She pulled the red bows from Curley's fur. She grabbed her broom and started sweeping.

"Patty the Pretty Poodle!" Elaine's voice rang out. "She's ready for her beauty treatments!"

Curley took a deep breath. She walked into the front room. It was time to do her job. She wished Lydia hadn't taken the bows out of her fur. But she understood. Lydia didn't want to get in trouble. Still, Curley wondered if she had looked pretty with the bows in her fur. She wished she had seen herself in a mirror.

"Good afternoon, Patty," Curley said.

But Patty wasn't listening. She was too busy eavesdropping on Felicia and Elaine.

"He's pure trouble," Elaine hissed. "Every year he cheats and never gets caught."

"One of these days," Felicia said calmly, "the truth will come out. We just have to do our jobs and let these things work out. They always do."

"But how can you stand the way he behaves in your salon?" Elaine squealed. "I don't know why you don't kick him right out!"

"Sometimes it's better to just find a way around trouble," Felicia said. "Now! Let's get going with making Pretty Patty even prettier!"

Felicia started toward the back room. But Elaine grabbed her arm.

"Felicia!" Elaine said. She seemed scared. "What do you think he'll do this year? Did you see the way he glared at Patty?"

Felicia didn't seem to know what to say.

Suddenly, all Curley could remember was Dennis standing by the electric box in the back alley!

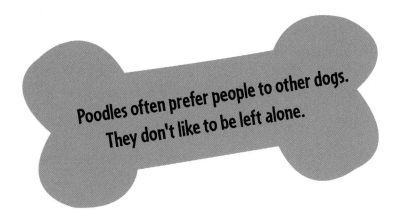

Poodles often prefer people to other dogs. They don't like to be left alone.

Chapter 6

Curley and Felicia stepped into the dark salon. It was another early morning.

"This has been a tiring week, hasn't it, Curley?" Felicia said. She turned on the lights.

They were starting extra early today. It was the day of the big show. Most dogs in the show would come into the salon today. There would be no time for anything but work.

"We can do it!" Curley barked to Felicia.

"Who's the best assistant ever?" Felicia laughed.

Curley barked.

"That's right! You are!" Felicia said. She gave Curley a crunchy treat. "Okay. Let's go see who's waiting out front."

Felicia was right. Their first customer was already waiting outside the front door.

"Good morning, Lady Red," Felicia said to a beautiful Irish Setter.

The gorgeous dog and its owner swept into the waiting room. Curley trotted up to the Setter and said hello. The day had begun.

The Irish Setter was followed by a Pug named Stanley. Then a German Shepherd named Hans. After Hans, a Pekingese named Sweet Peaches came in. Felicia and Curley never stopped until lunch. They took a short break, and then the bell above the front door rang again.

"Lionel is waiting!" thundered Dennis's voice.

Curley heard Felicia sigh. Then she walked out to the front room.

"Hello," Felicia said. "We're ready for you."

Curley scooted over to Lionel.

"What took you so long?" said Lionel. "I need water and a small snack. Nothing fattening. I've been working all morning. I'm exhausted. And yet . . . I still look good."

Lionel strutted across the floor. Curley filled a fresh dish with water. She carried a piece of rawhide over to Lionel.

"I'm sure you have been working hard!" Curley said to the big dog. "It must be tiring to get ready for such a big show."

I look good.

"You have no idea!" Lionel said. He never actually looked at Curley. His nose was always too high in the air to look that far down. "I've been walking and sitting and posing for hours. Exhausting! Just take me back to the table. I need to relax!"

"Right this way," Curley said.

"Have you been busy?" Dennis asked Felicia.

"Actually, we have," Felicia said. She looked at Dennis. She was surprised he would ask about anything other than himself or Lionel.

"I'm sure," snapped Dennis. "All those wannabes that won't-ever-bes! Every dog owner in town wants to beat Lionel. Some of them actually think they stand a chance! Ha! They think a little grooming will do the trick, but Lionel is unbeatable!"

Felicia put her head down. She didn't even want to look at Dennis.

"Well, it looks like Curley has already taken Lionel to the back room," Felicia said. "Make yourself comfortable. I'll get right to work."

Felicia headed to the back room. Then she stopped. She returned to her desk and closed her date book. She put it in a drawer and locked it. Dennis watched her. He tried to make it look like he was smiling. But he wasn't.

Felicia stood in front of Lionel. She looked at the dog for a minute. Then she started at the top. She gave the big dog the full treatment. She cleaned his eyes and nose. She combed and brushed him. She did his nails. She brushed his teeth! She worked all her magic. Curley ran back and forth. Lionel never stopped asking for things. At last Felicia was done. Curley was exhausted.

But when Lionel stepped down off the table, even Curley had to admire him. He was a handsome dog.

Lionel didn't stop to say thank you. He didn't look at Felicia or Curley. He just held his head and strutted into the front room.

"Best in Show!" Dennis said as soon as Lionel appeared. "It's a cinch!"

Just then, the bell rang again. Patty and

Elaine walked into the salon. The room fell silent. Elaine stared at Lionel. Dennis stared at Patty. Lionel stared at Patty, and Patty stared at Lionel. Lionel puffed out his cheeks. Patty's tail tucked between her legs just a bit.

"Okay, then!" Felicia finally exclaimed.

How Can You Tell if a Dog Is Feeling Stress?

Dogs can't talk to us. So humans have to read their body language. When dogs are feeling stressed, they will "tell" you in different ways. Here are some things to look for: shaking, yawning, refusing to eat or open the mouth, licking lips, drooling, panting, hiding, avoiding eye contact, tucking the tail between the legs, hiding, and of course, biting or growling. Every dog shows stress in its own way. When you get to know a dog, you will learn the signs that dog gives to let you know they're stressed!

"Thank you, Dennis, and welcome, Elaine. Let's keep moving! Busy day! Busy day!"

Dennis snarled. He and Lionel circled around Elaine and Patty, trying to make them nervous.

"Good luck," Dennis said. Then he laughed. Finally, the nasty pair left the shop.

Felicia hurried Elaine and Patty into the back room. But Curley stayed and watched Dennis and Lionel. They walked down the sidewalk slowly. They stared back at the salon. Curley was sure they were up to something. But she had a job to do.

Curley hurried back to Patty.

"You look beautiful today, Patty!" Curley said. She tried to make the other Poodle comfortable. But she could tell Patty was nervous. So was Curley. Lionel and Dennis had made everyone nervous.

Felicia was hard at work. Patty was getting the extra-curly treatment. It was a technique only Felicia used. She had invented it. She put dozens of tiny heated curlers in Patty's fur. This was to make every curl perfect! Each curler was attached to the main machine by a cord. The machine was plugged into the wall. Curley stepped carefully around the machine. Felicia had warned Curley many times about the machine. "Be extra careful around all these electrical wires!"

"Once I get all the curlers in," Felicia said, "we'll set the timer. It's important that they stay in for just the right amount of time and at just the right temperature."

Curley was so tired now, she could barely stand up. She decided it was a good time to slip away. She would just take a short nap in the back alley. Then she'd be ready to face the rest of the day. She quietly stepped out of the room. She pushed the door open into the alley. She walked to her corner. She was just turning around three times when she heard something jingle.

She spun around. She saw that same flash

she had seen before. But this time the flash fell to the ground. Then there was a POP! The lights inside the salon went black.

Curley heard a scream followed by a howl!

What happened?

Chapter 7

Curley ran back inside. At the same time, the emergency generator switched on. It made a big roaring noise. The lights flickered on. Curley raced into the back room in time to see Felicia running to Patty.

"Oh, no! Oh, no!" cried Felicia.

"What? What happened?" Elaine screamed. "Patty! Are you okay?"

Something smelled bad. Curley couldn't tell what it was. Then she realized there was smoke all around Patty. Felicia pushed away the blow-dryers. She started pulling out the curlers as fast as she could.

"*AAAUUGGHH!*" Elaine screeched in horror.

With every curler that Felicia removed, a clump of fur fell out. The fur that remained was brownish yellow and completely frizzy. Patty's fur was totally fried!

"No! No! No!" Elaine cried.

Patty stood absolutely still. Her eyes were wide open. She was too scared to look at her own fur.

"Are you in pain?" Curley barked to Patty.

Patty's eyes shifted down to the little Poodle. She gave a small shake of her head.

"Okay," said Curley. "Well, that's the important thing!"

But Patty didn't look comforted. She looked terrified.

"What have you done?" Elaine screamed. She scooped up handfuls of Patty's fur from the floor. "My champion is fried to a crisp!"

"I don't understand!" Felicia uttered. "There's never been a problem with our electricity. I'm so sorry!"

"But Patty is okay!" Curley barked softly. "Her fur will grow back! The important thing is she didn't get hurt!"

"Hush!" Elaine snapped at Curley.

Just then, Lydia arrived. Curley was still

Fur Pete's Sake!
Poodles don't actually have fur. They have hair. That means it never stops growing. It's also why many people who are allergic to most dogs can live with Poodles. Because there's no fur to make them sneeze!

Poor Patty!

staring at Elaine. She had never been yelled at like that. It felt awful.

Lydia rushed over to Curley. She scooped her up. She looked around the room, trying to figure out what was going on.

"What happened?" Lydia finally asked.

"What happened?" Elaine screamed. "What happened? I'll tell you what happened. This machine shorted out the electric system, and my Best in Show is now a bald french-fried Poodle!"

Lydia held Curley tight. She shuffled back into a corner.

"This has never happened before, Elaine! I don't understand!" Felicia said the same thing over and over. It was like she was in shock. She kept working on Patty. She checked every inch of her skin for burns.

"I know it doesn't help at the moment . . ." said Felicia. She tried to sound calm, but it wasn't working. It made Curley's heart hurt.

"But," Felicia finally added, "it doesn't look like Patty was injured."

"*AAAUUGGHH!*" Elaine screamed again.

Patty jumped off the table. She squeezed

herself beneath it. She was trying to hide. She didn't want anyone to see her.

"She can't even bear to look at herself!" Elaine cried.

Lydia took a deep breath. Curley looked up at her.

"We all have to calm down," the girl said. "Patty's fur will grow back. She will be Best in Show next year. The most important thing is that she isn't hurt."

Lydia's calm, quiet voice seemed to work. Everyone stopped and looked at her.

"The other most important thing," Lydia continued, "is that we have to keep Lionel from winning."

"How are we supposed to do that?" Felicia asked. She sounded totally defeated. "Patty was the only dog that had a chance against Lionel."

Elaine just sobbed into a handful of burned fur.

Curley was still staring at Lydia. Then she saw a smile sneak across Lydia's face.

"What are you smiling about?" asked Felicia. "This is a disaster!"

"I have a plan," Lydia said. "Curley."

Elaine looked up from the burnt fur. Felicia stared at Lydia and Curley. Then she and Elaine began to laugh.

It was more than Curley could bear. She leaped out of Lydia's arms and ran to the back alley.

Some people believe that Poodles are the smartest of all dog breeds.

Chapter 8

Curley ran to her corner. She covered her head with her paws. She could feel herself shaking. She felt worse than she had ever felt before.

She heard footsteps. She knew it was Lydia.

"Hey, pretty dog," Lydia said softly. The girl sat down next to Curley. She was quiet for a minute. "Felicia didn't mean to laugh. She's just really upset right now. She loves you very much. She knows you're a beautiful dog. She just thinks of you as beautiful on the inside. We have to show her you're beautiful on the outside, too."

Curley whimpered. She wanted to disappear.

"This is our chance, Curley," Lydia said.

"You're going to take Patty's place in the show, and we're going to win that trophy!"

"I could *never* take Patty's place," Curley whispered.

"I actually checked the breed standards recently," Lydia said. "You're small, but not too small to compete as a Standard Poodle. Come on, Curley. We don't have a lot of time. Give me that Curley-can-do bark!"

Curley suddenly realized what Lydia had said. Lydia had actually checked to see if she would be able to compete! She had actually thought about Curley competing before this whole disaster! Lydia believed in her!

Curley couldn't let her down. Curley lifted her head and barked.

Lydia laughed. She hugged Curley. Curley walked back into the salon.

"Would you excuse us?" Lydia asked Elaine, Felicia, and Patty. "Curley will be ready soon. We just need the room to ourselves."

Felicia and Elaine didn't say a word. They were too stunned to speak. Patty crawled out of the room on her belly.

The door shut. Lydia turned to Curley.

"Let's get busy!" she said.

Curley jumped up on the table.

Lydia brushed and buffed and combed and primped. Curley was impressed. She could tell Lydia had been watching Felicia carefully. She knew a lot of the salon owner's tricks for making dogs beautiful.

Thank you, Lydia.

"Thank you," Curley woofed softly.

Lydia was curling her eyelashes.

"Ssshhh," said Lydia. The girl was completely focused. "I . . . just . . . have . . . to . . . finish. . . ."

She backed away slowly from Curley. It was clear she was looking at the whole picture now. She had attended to every detail. It was time to see if it had worked.

Curley's eyes were wide open. She stared at the girl. She tried to find some sign. Finally, Lydia's eyes started to sparkle. A smile crept onto her face.

"Red is definitely your color!" she said.

Lydia rolled the big mirror around so that Curley could look at herself. It wasn't possible!

Who Usually Wins at a Dog Show?
One of the biggest dog shows in America is the Westminster Kennel Club Dog Show. It happens every year in New York City. The list of winners proves that lots of different breeds can win Best in Show. But dogs in the terrier group have won the most often. Out of the 100 times that the Best in Show award has been given, a terrier has won 47 times!

She didn't recognize the dog in the mirror.

"You're beautiful, aren't you?" Lydia said.

Curley couldn't believe her eyes.

"Felicia? Elaine? Patty?" Lydia called.

The three hurried into the back room.

Elaine's hand flew to her mouth. Felicia's jaw dropped. Patty whimpered.

"Don't worry, Patty." Lydia laughed. "It's Curley. It's really Curley!"

"Amazing!" Felicia whispered. "Why didn't I ever see it before?"

It was like music to Curley's ears. Felicia was finally looking at her like she was a show dog.

Curley was beautiful, and she felt it. She could feel it inside and out!

But Elaine was not as happy as everyone else.

"Curley is going to replace Pretty Patty?" She started sobbing again. "Curley is going to be a winner? How could this happen? What went wrong?"

Felicia looked away from Curley. Curley

knew she felt guilty about what had happened to Patty. She felt like it was her fault.

"I have to go check the electric box," Felicia said.

The words "electric box" jolted Curley into action.

The electric box! Curley had completely forgotten what she'd seen. She forgot what she had heard just before the lights went out. Curley jumped down from the table. She barked loudly.

"Follow me, Felicia!" Curley barked over and over. Curley led everyone out to the back alley.

Suddenly, Curley knew exactly what that flash had been. She also knew exactly what had happened and who had done it!

Chapter 9

"Curley!" Felicia called. "What's wrong? Slow down!"

It was a mad dash to the back alley.

"Curley!" Lydia called. "Don't forget! You're all fixed up for the show. Don't get dirty!"

Curley had forgotten. She tried to settle down, but she had to show Felicia what she knew.

"Are you scared?" Felicia asked as she ran after Curley. "Don't be scared. You can do this! You'll be great."

"I'm not scared," barked Curley. "Look! Look under the electric box!"

"The box is open!" Felicia exclaimed. "Who opened it? Somebody was doing something back here!"

Curley pawed at the ground. She tried hard not to make a mess of her painted nails.

Felicia looked down. She gasped as she stared at the thing that was lying on the ground underneath the electric box.

Curley put her head down and gently picked up the metal trinket.

"It's Dennis's collection of Best in Show charms!" Elaine squeaked.

"Dennis!" Felicia said. She stared in disbelief. "He blew the fuse box and caused a power surge!"

Elaine looked at Patty. She stared at her bald patches.

"He did this on purpose!" Elaine sobbed. "I never thought he would go this far!"

"He'd do anything to win," Felicia said sadly.

"Not this time!" Lydia exclaimed. "We need to get to the gym. He's not going to get away with this."

"I'm calling the police!" Elaine said. She was mad now. She was done crying. Now she

65

was going to make sure Dennis got punished!

"Meet us at the show!" Felicia called out.

Felicia and Lydia rushed toward the front door. Curley stopped in front of Patty.

"It's okay," whispered Patty. "Thanks for

What's It Like in the Ring?

A lot happens when a dog steps into the ring at a dog show. Judges look at the way the dog walks and runs. They watch how the dog responds to its trainer. Then they study each dog individually. The judges check a dog's teeth, head, and expression. They check the fur and body condition. A dog has to be good with people (and other dogs) to stay calm during competition. Here's what every champion knows: Manners are important!

doing this. Go give it your all!"

Curley touched her nose to Patty's nose.

"Just this year," Curley said. "Next year, you'll be back, and you'll win for sure!"

"Curley!" Lydia called.

Curley ran to Lydia. She was ready!

★ ★ ★ ★ ★

They were late. The doors to the gym were already closed when they arrived.

"You're too late to enter," called a guard.

Lydia didn't miss a beat. She turned on the tears. "Please, mister! This is the most important day of my life. We had a terrible accident and got here as soon as we could!"

The guard looked around. Lydia didn't stop.

"Please don't do this to my dog, mister!" Lydia cried. "She's been through so much in her life—"

"Okay! Okay!" the guard finally said. "Hurry up! Before anyone sees me letting you in!"

He opened the door just wide enough for

Lydia, Felicia, and Curley to slip through.

Curley froze. She could see the show ring a short distance away. She was surrounded by beautiful dogs. But this time, she was one of them. It was so exciting! She could barely breathe!

"We have a last-minute replacement," said a booming voice over the loudspeaker. Curley jumped. "Curley the Poodle and her trainer, Lydia!"

"That's us!" Lydia shouted.

The next thing Curley knew, she was in the center of the ring. She pranced beside Lydia. They ran all around the ring. She did everything just like she had seen other dogs do for so many years.

But this time, the spotlight was on Curley!

Chapter 10

The crowd roared. The more Curley pranced, the louder the crowd cheered. She held her head high. She lifted her paws proudly. She stayed in the spotlight.

This is the most fun I've ever had! Curley thought. *This is my best day!*

Lydia stopped. Curley stopped on a dime. She was so glad she had watched so many shows with Felicia. There was nothing she didn't know about how show dogs were supposed to act.

The judges walked up to her. They looked her up and down.

"She's small," said a woman in a black skirt.

"I like to think of her as petite," Lydia said with a smile.

"Very spirited!" said another judge.

"Curley is the best dog ever," Lydia said proudly.

"Woof!" Curley barked softly.

The judges laughed. The crowd cheered. They loved the way Curley seemed to enjoy being the center of attention.

One of the judges raised her arm. Curley and Lydia ran another lap.

Curley looked to the side of the ring. Felicia was cheering more than anyone. "Go, Curley!" Felicia called.

Curley tilted her head to Felicia. Felicia laughed.

At last, it was time for Lydia and Curley to take their seats. There were many other dogs that still had to compete. It was all a blur. Curley tried to pay attention to the dogs in the ring, but her heart was pounding.

"You were great!" Lydia laughed.

Felicia pushed her way through the crowd. She sat down next to them. She put her hands on either side of Curley's head.

"You are my Best in Show! It doesn't matter who gets a trophy!" Felicia said.

Curley licked her hand.

Suddenly, the announcer said, "Please welcome our returning champion, Lionel, and his trainer, Dennis. . . ."

Curley, Lydia, and Felicia all turned toward the ring.

Curley's stomach flipped. Dennis was glaring right at her.

"Look at them! Dennis looks like he has nothing to be ashamed about!" cried Lydia.

The crowd applauded. Lionel was a stunning dog, after all.

"Don't worry. He'll pay for what he did," Felicia said. Then she looked around the crowd. Curley knew she was looking for Elaine.

"What's taking them so long?" Curley woofed softly. "The competition is almost over."

Lionel trotted around the ring with his head high. He was confident. He looked like he was King of the World.

Dennis sneered at Felicia every time he passed them.

Felicia got up and walked to the door. She was searching for Elaine.

Lionel stood for the judges. Curley watched every move. It was clear the judges were impressed with him. They gave the signal for Lionel to make his final circle around the arena. As he did, the crowd cheered loudly.

Curley's heart grew heavy.

The crowd likes him best, thought Curley. *Dennis did a terrible thing to Patty, but they're going to win anyway.*

"It's time for the final showing," said the voice on the loudspeaker. "Ladies and gentlemen, show your appreciation for all our competitors before we award the Best in Show!"

The crowd began to cheer.

"Come on, Curley," whispered Lydia. "You haven't come this far to lose your confidence now!"

Curley got up. She fell into the long line of dogs. One after another they followed each other around the ring.

The crowd cheered louder as all the dogs took one more turn around the ring. Then they all had to line up. Curley was right in the middle of the longest line of beautiful dogs she had ever seen.

They all stood tall and proud. Curley held her head high. She was doing it for Lydia and Felicia and Patty. She was doing it for herself.

The judges walked up and down the line one last time. Then they walked back to the table where a huge trophy sat. The crowd grew quiet. Out of the corner of her eye, Curley saw Lionel. He was five dogs down from her. He was sure he would win.

"Ladies and gentlemen, please congratulate this year's Best in Show . . ."

Curley couldn't breathe. There was a buzzing in her ears. She thought she might just fall over. But suddenly, the buzzing went away.

"Curley the Poodle and her trainer, Lydia!"

Curley looked up at Lydia. She stared at her with her eyes wide. Lydia was staring back at Curley. Neither of them moved.

The crowd cheered so loudly that Curley couldn't hear anything else.

Lydia started shaking her head. Then she started laughing. Finally, she put her hand on Curley's head. "Come on!" she shouted. "Let's get your trophy!"

Curley was walking, but she couldn't feel

her paws. It felt more like she was floating. The judges shook Lydia's hand. They patted Curley on the head.

"This dog is Best in Show — inside and out!" called the voice over the loudspeaker. The crowd went wild. They agreed!

Curley turned in a circle and barked to the crowd. That was when she saw Felicia standing by the door. Elaine and Patty were with her. They were jumping up and down and cheering. Then Curley saw something even more surprising.

Two police officers walked up to Dennis. They grabbed him and turned him around. They marched him out of the gym. As he passed Felicia and Elaine, he looked away. Lionel hung his head.

"Hooray!" barked Curley.

"Finally!" cried Lydia. "Everybody got what they deserved!"

Felicia, Elaine, and Pretty Patty rushed up to Lydia and Curley.

"Thank you, Lydia!" Felicia said. "Thank

you for seeing what I didn't see! As soon as you get a little older, I hope you'll work with us more. You're part of the family now!"

Lydia squeezed Curley. "Did you hear that, Curley? We're family!"

"You're a star!" Felicia said to Curley with a smile.

"A star is born!" Lydia exclaimed.

And everyone agreed!

We're family!

I hope you enjoy the stories.
Judy Spolarich
Page 162

God Answers
Prayers
Military Edition

Allison Bottke

with **Cheryll Hutchings** and **Jennifer Devlin**

HARVEST HOUSE PUBLISHERS

EUGENE, OREGON

To protect the privacy of the individuals involved in the following stories, the names have been changed when deemed appropriate.

Cover by Left Coast Design, Portland, Oregon

Back cover photo is a DoD photo by Staff Sgt. Eddie L. Bradley, U.S. Air Force. (Released)

All stories submitted use military jargon, phrases, and designations as given by the author.

GOD ANSWERS PRAYERS—MILITARY EDITION
Copyright © 2005 by Allison Bottke
Published by Harvest House Publishers
Eugene, Oregon 97402
www.harvesthousepublishers.com

Library of Congress Cataloging-in-Publication Data

God answers prayers / [edited by] Allison Bottke with Cheryll Hutchings and Jennifer Devlin.— Military ed.
    p. cm. — (God answers prayers)
  ISBN-13: 978-0-7369-1666-0 (pbk.)
  ISBN-10: 0-7369-1666-0
  1. Prayer—Christianity.   2. Soldiers—Religious life.   I. Bottke, Allison   II. Hutchings, Cheryll.   III. Devlin, Jennifer.   IV. Series.
  BV220.G595   2005
  242'.68—dc22   2005012407

Printed in the United States of America

05   06   07   08   09   10   11   12   / VP-CF /   10   9   8   7   6   5   4   3   2   1